OCTONAUTS™

and the Colossal Squid

SIMON AND SCHUSTER

The Octonauts were voyaging through deep, dark waters when Captain Barnacles spotted something floating in the gloom.
"I wonder what those little lights are up ahead," he said.

The Octopod moved in for a closer look. BANG!
"Captain!" cried Dashi. "Something's got us!"

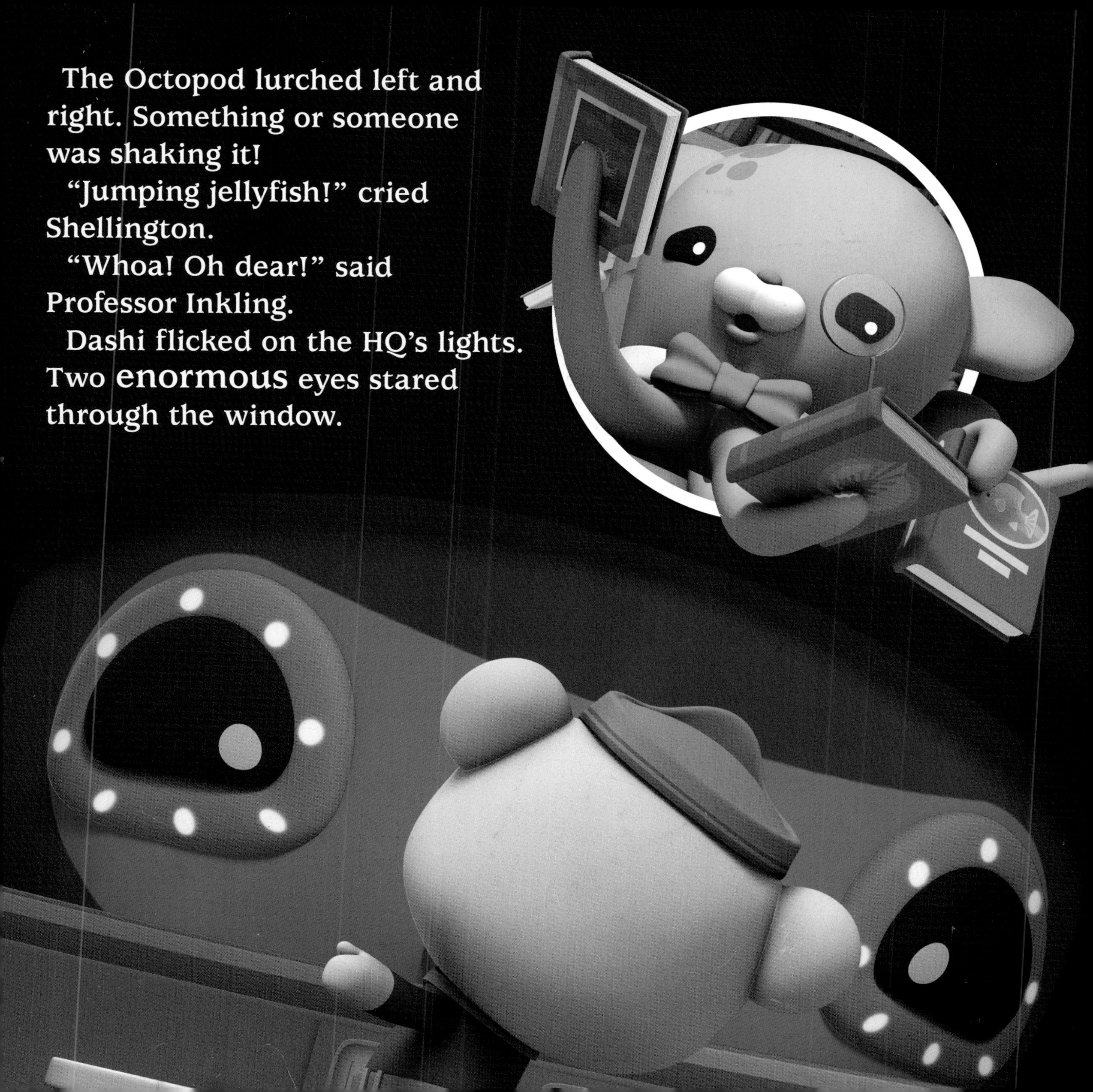

The Octopod lurched left and right. Something or someone was shaking it!

"Jumping jellyfish!" cried Shellington.

"Whoa! Oh dear!" said Professor Inkling.

Dashi flicked on the HQ's lights. Two **enormous** eyes stared through the window.

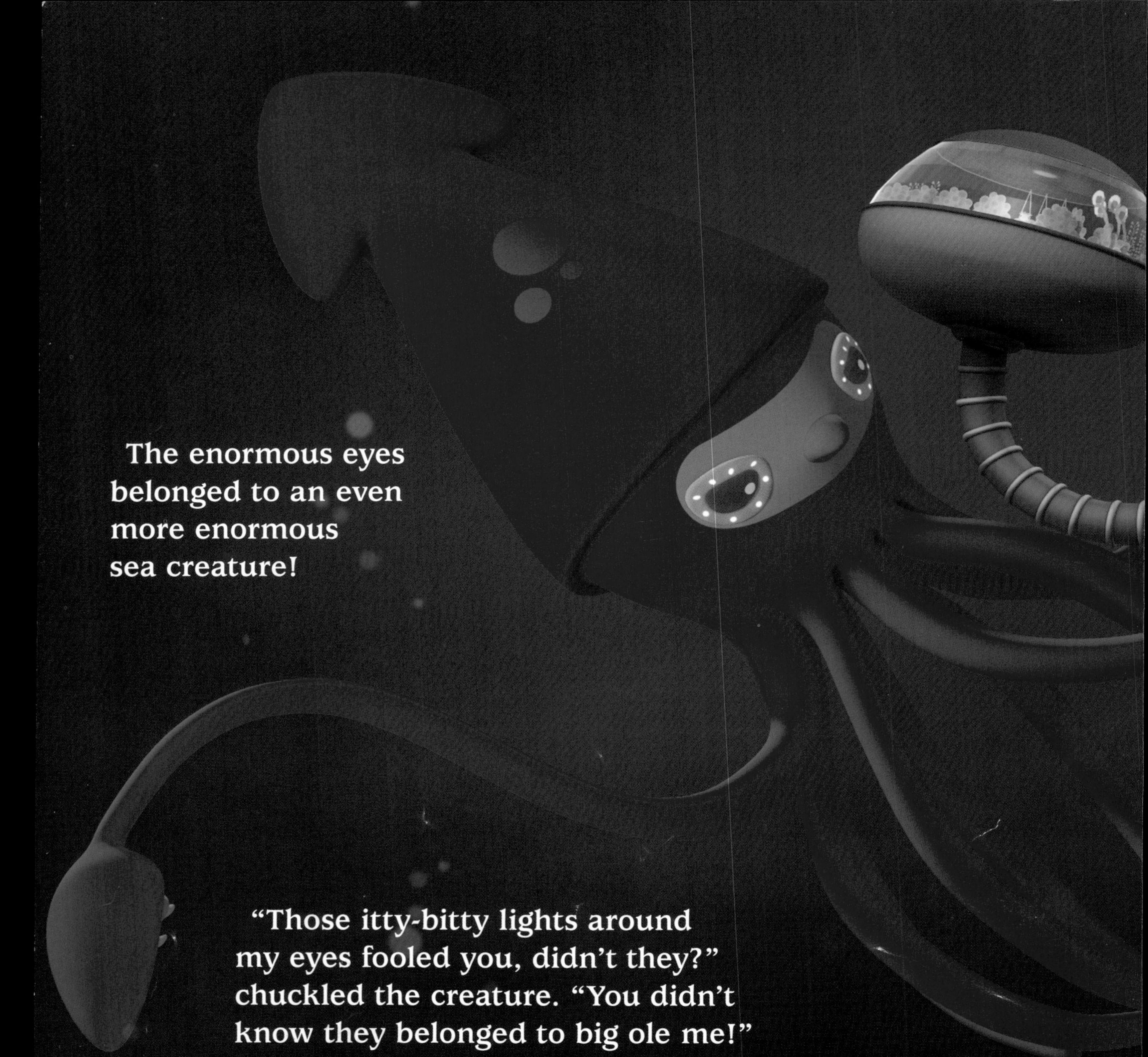

The enormous eyes belonged to an even more enormous sea creature!

"Those itty-bitty lights around my eyes fooled you, didn't they?" chuckled the creature. "You didn't know they belonged to big ole me!"

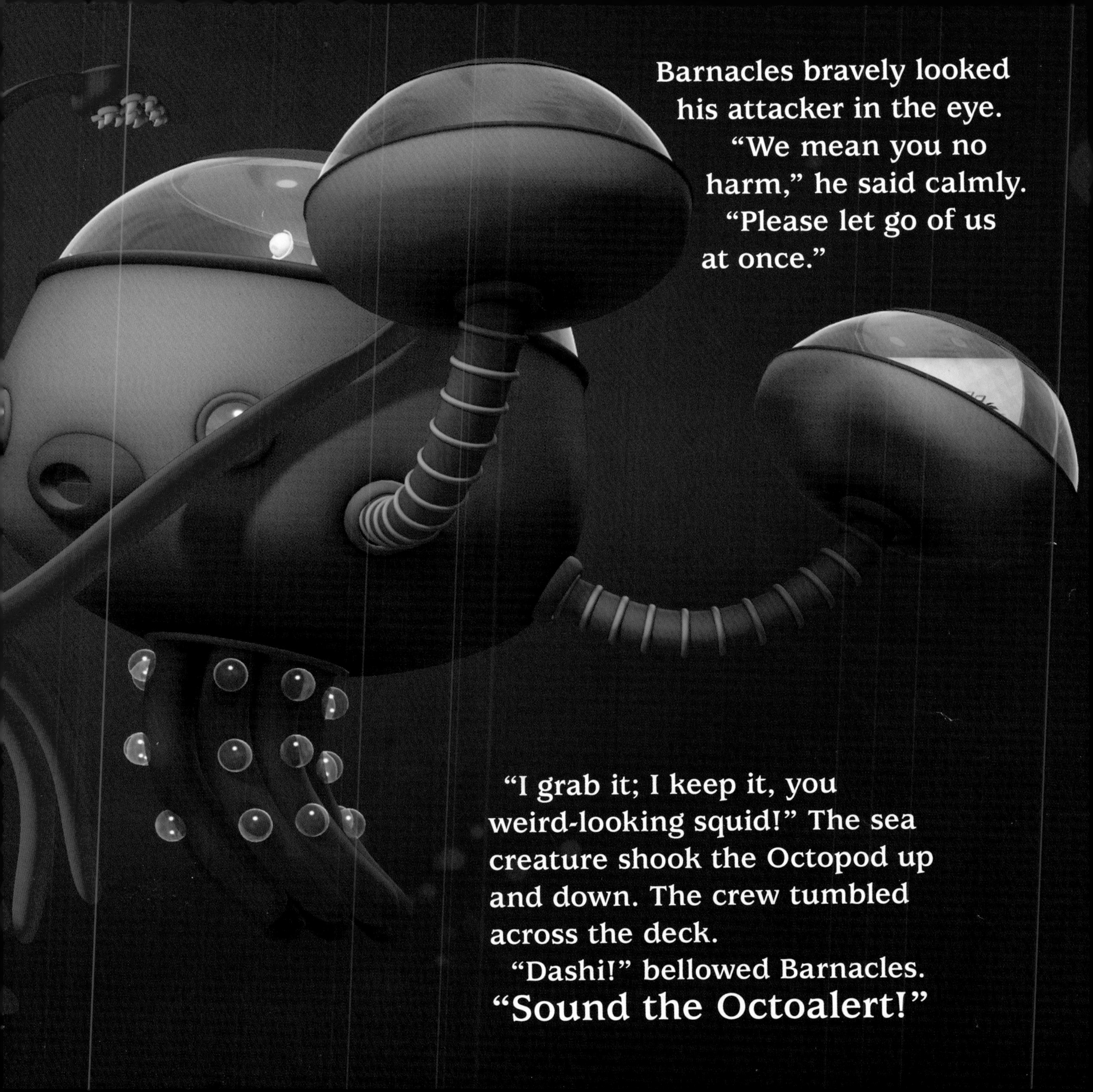

Barnacles bravely looked his attacker in the eye. "We mean you no harm," he said calmly. "Please let go of us at once."

"I grab it; I keep it, you weird-looking squid!" The sea creature shook the Octopod up and down. The crew tumbled across the deck.

"Dashi!" bellowed Barnacles. "Sound the Octoalert!"

“Octonauts

to the HQ!”

"Shellington!" cried the Captain.
"Any idea what has grabbed us?"
Shellington said, "It's a colossal squid!"
"It's like my cousin the giant squid," nodded Inkling, "only bigger!"
The colossal squid stopped shaking the Octopod. Phew!
Now it was crushing it instead!

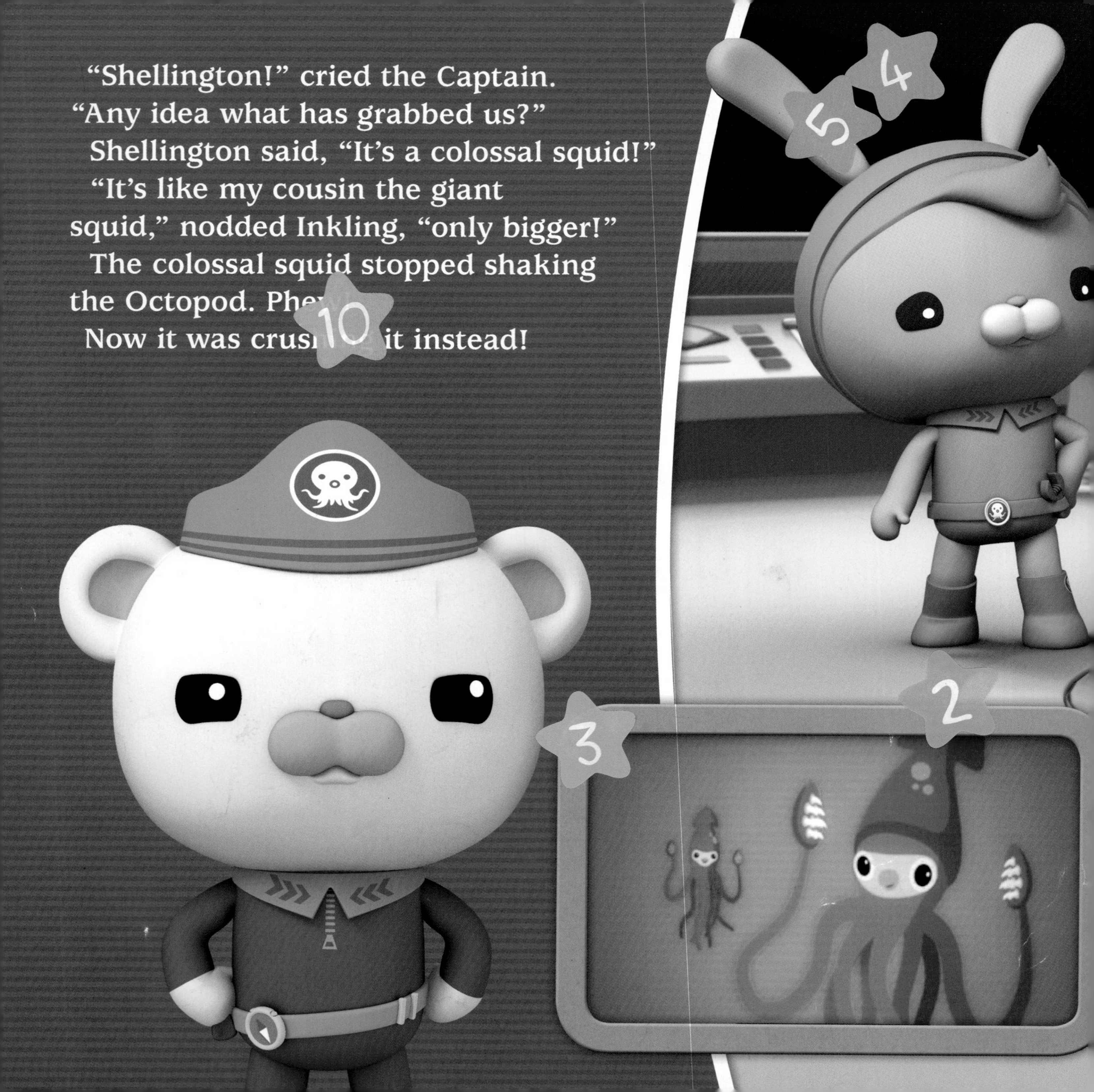

The crew needed to match the squid tentacle for tentacle. Tweak and Professor Inkling had just the thing.

"Wearing this Tentacle Suit," explained Tweak, "Professor Inkling will be able to move the arms of the Octopod as if they were his own tentacles."

The Octonauts grinned. The Professor was an expert at tentacle wrestling!

Professor Inkling started grappling with the colossal squid. It was a tough battle. The HQ windows went black.

"Ink cloud!" said Shellington. "A classic squid move."

"Oh my!" gasped the Professor. "He's got his hooks into us!"

FACT: SUPER TENTACLES

A colossal squid has sharp hooks on the ends of its tentacles.

Barnacles and Kwazii put on their deep sea diving suits. They had to pry the colossal squid's hooks out before he dragged the Octopod down any further.

The Octonauts tried using their paws to lift off the squid's tentacles.

"Grrr..." growled the Captain. "For every hook we loosen, two more move into place."

Just then, Dashi's voice came over the radio.

"Captain," she cried. "There's something heading straight for us!"

"It's a sperm whale," added Shellington,

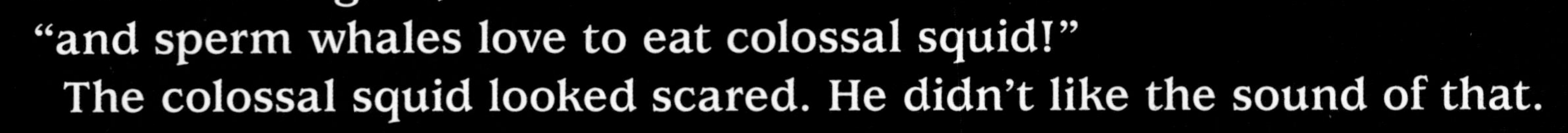

"and sperm whales love to eat colossal squid!"

The colossal squid looked scared. He didn't like the sound of that.

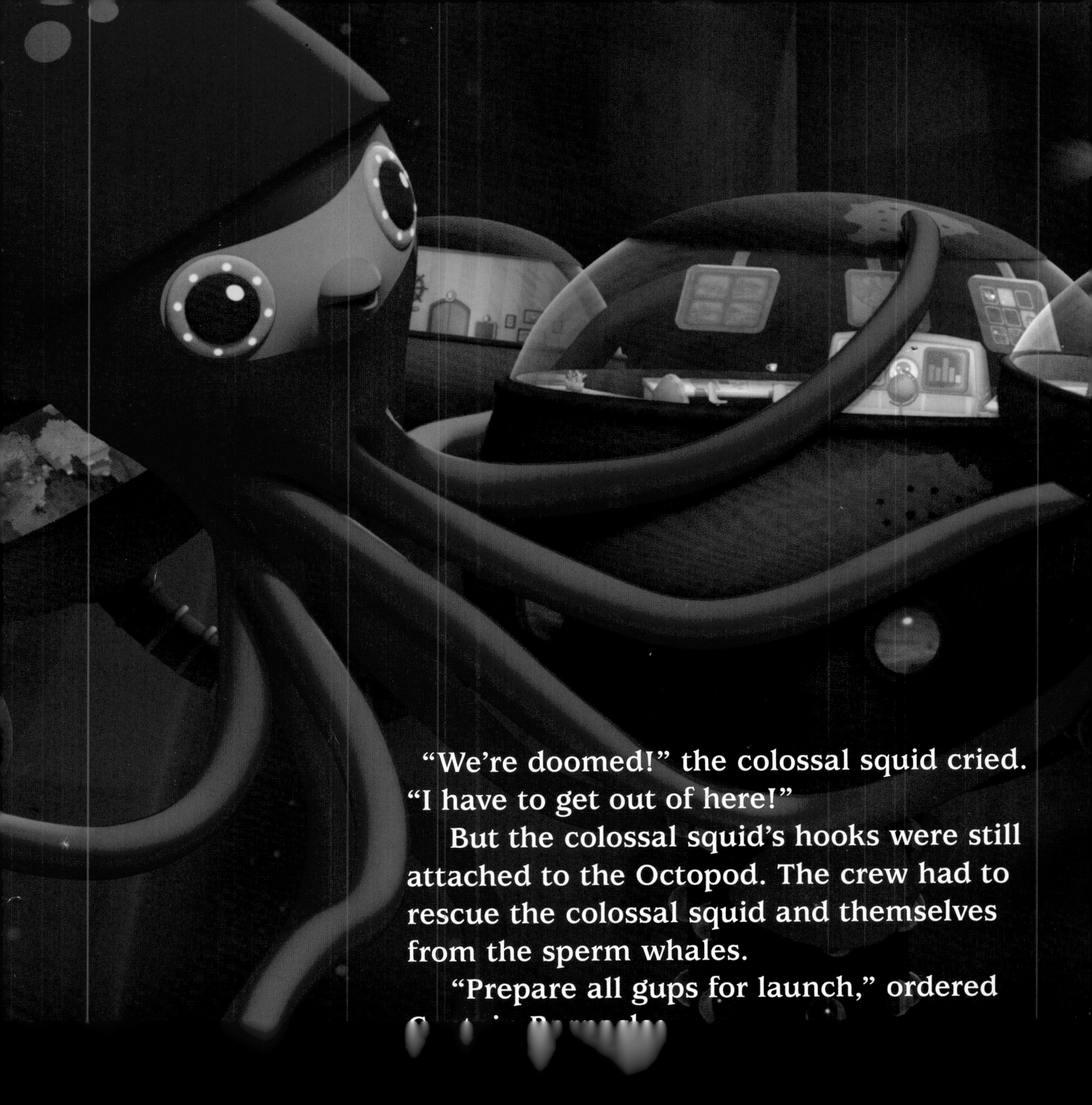

“We’re doomed!” the colossal squid cried. “I have to get out of here!”

But the colossal squid’s hooks were still attached to the Octopod. The crew had to rescue the colossal squid and themselves from the sperm whales.

“Prepare all gups for launch,” ordered Captain Barnacles.

The Octonauts scrambled into the gups and attached their towlines to the Octopod. Together they powered through the water, dragging the Octopod and the colossal squid behind them.

The whales followed.

"There you are, my colossal dinner!" called the whale leader.

"Don't worry," Shellington said. "Sperm whales breathe air. Sooner or later they'll have to swim back up to the surface to breathe."

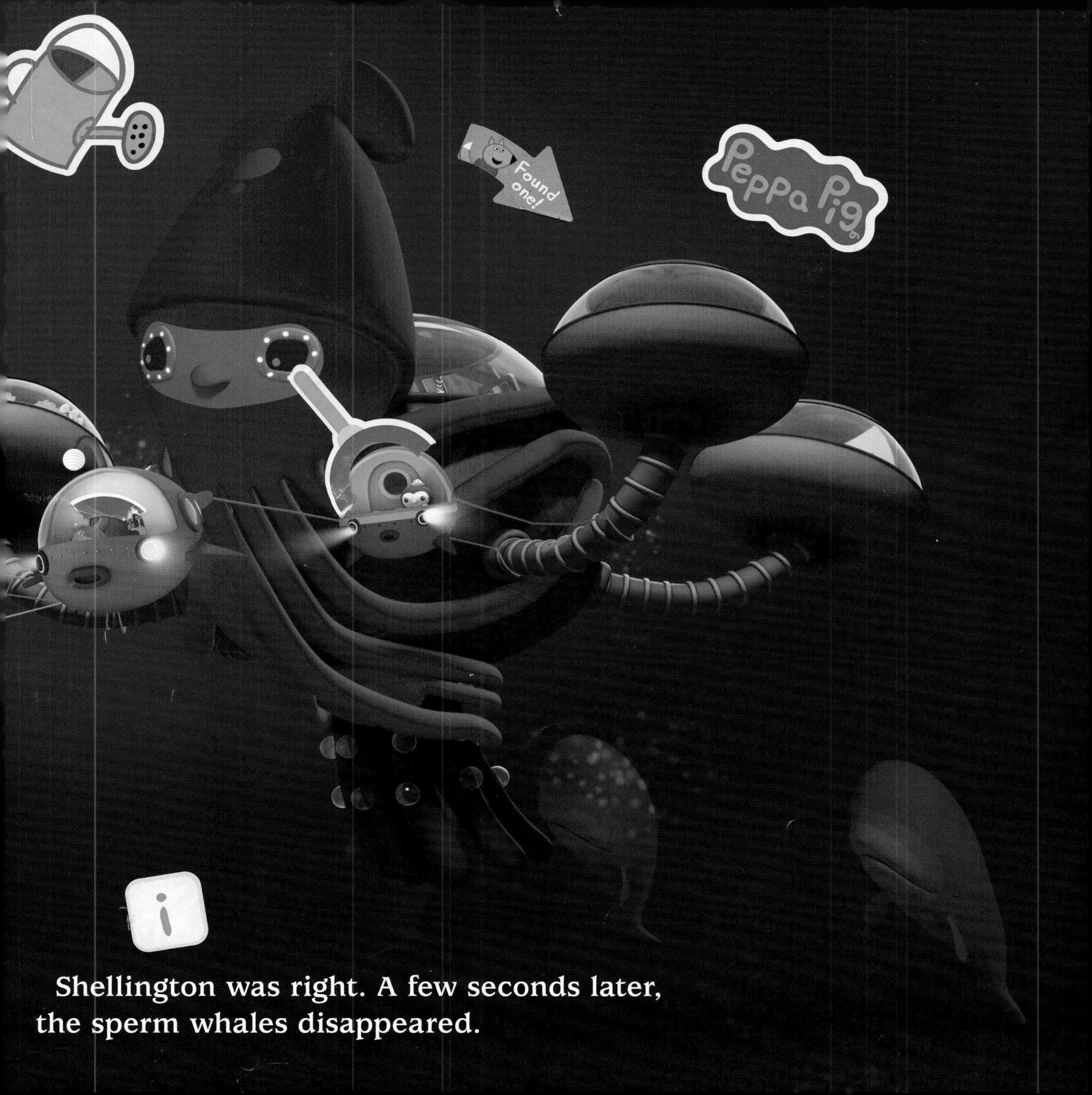

Shellington was right. A few seconds later, the sperm whales disappeared.

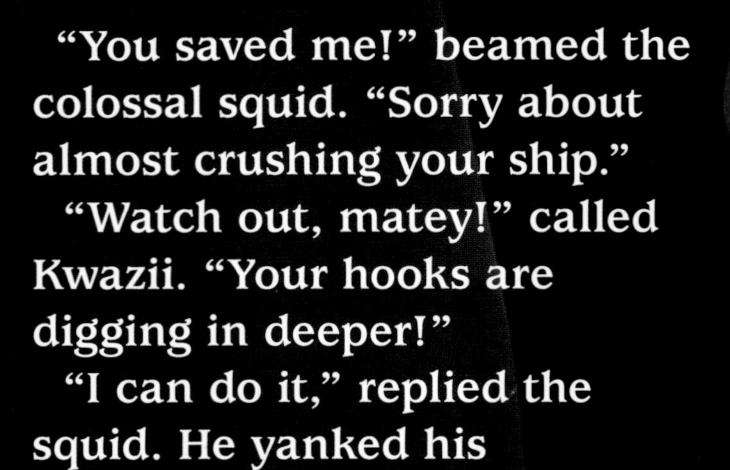

"You saved me!" beamed the colossal squid. "Sorry about almost crushing your ship."

"Watch out, matey!" called Kwazii. "Your hooks are digging in deeper!"

"I can do it," replied the squid. He yanked his tentacles as hard as he could.

CRACK!

The squid accidentally snapped an arm off the Octopod!

The garden pod sunk down into the abyss.

"Oh no!" cried Dashi. "Tunip and the Vegimals are in there!"

"Everybody dive!" instructed the Captain.

Still attached to the colossal squid, the gups plunged after the pod, but it disappeared into the darkness.

"I can see it!" bellowed the colossal squid.

FACT: SQUID VISION

The colossal squid's giant eyes help it to see in the dark.

With his squid vision, the colossal squid quickly spotted the pod.

"Hurry!" he called, "they're heading for some sharp rocks."

"Grab them if you can!" urged Barnacles.

The gigantic sea creature reached into the gloom.

"Got it!" he cried.

The Octonauts worked together to unhook their new friend. Next, the squid fixed the garden pod back onto the Octopod. "I think this calls for a tentacle bump!" said Professor Inkling.

Everyone chuckled. It had to be the most colossal high-five ever!

CAPTAIN'S LOG

Calling all Octonauts! Who would believe a colossal squid could be as big as the Octopod? The enormous creature was great at grabbing, but he had a hard time letting go. It took all of our ocean skills to avoid a tentacled catastrophe!

CAPTAIN BARNACLES

FACT FILE: THE COLOSSAL SQUID

- The colossal squid has the largest eyes in the animal kingdom.
- Its eyes have glowing dots all around the edge. Scientists think this helps the squid attract prey.
- Only the colossal squid has three-pronged hooks at the end of its tentacles.

The colossal squid is an undersea giant with eight swirling arms and two mega-tentacles. Stretching up to 14 metres long, it is the biggest known squid in the ocean.

It lives in the Midnight Zone.

It eats fish and squid.

Discover an ocean full of brand new Octonauts books!

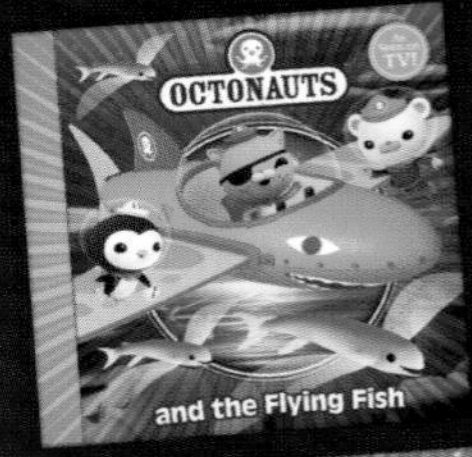

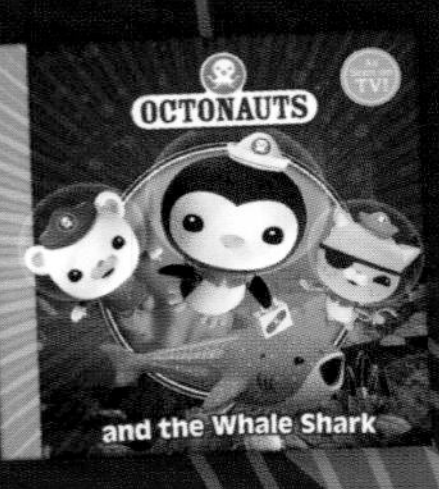

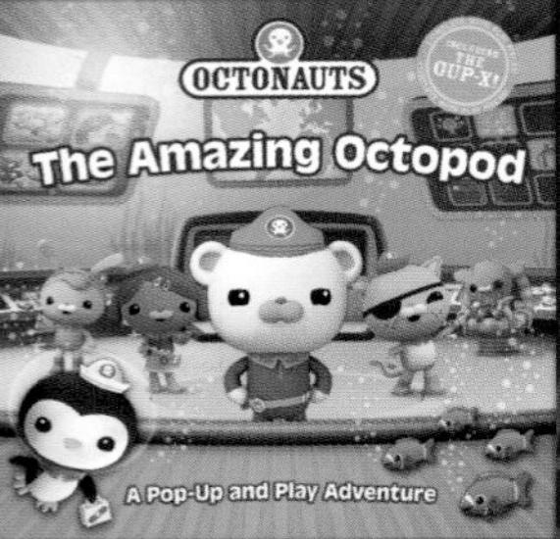

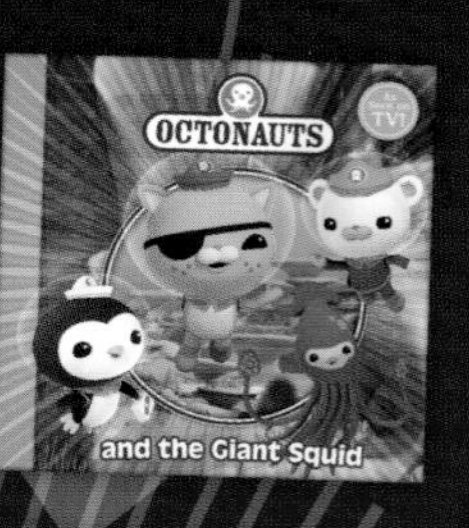

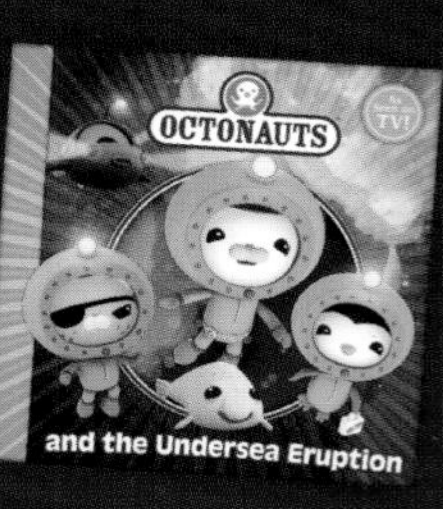

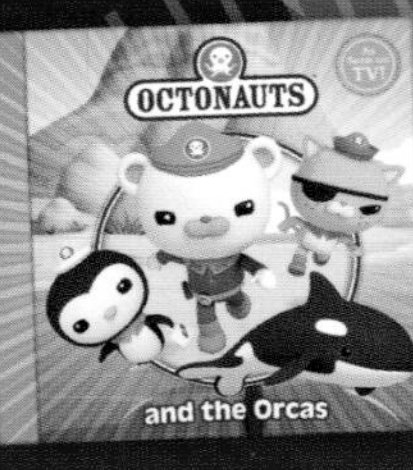

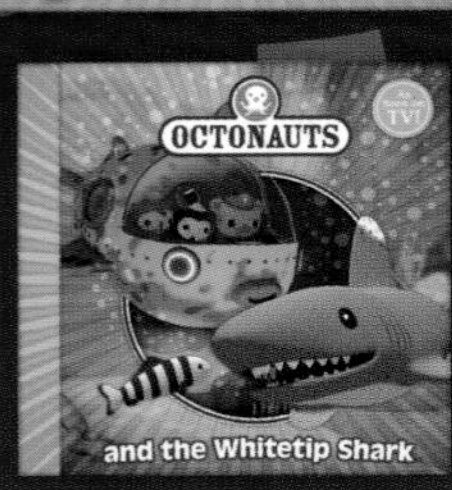

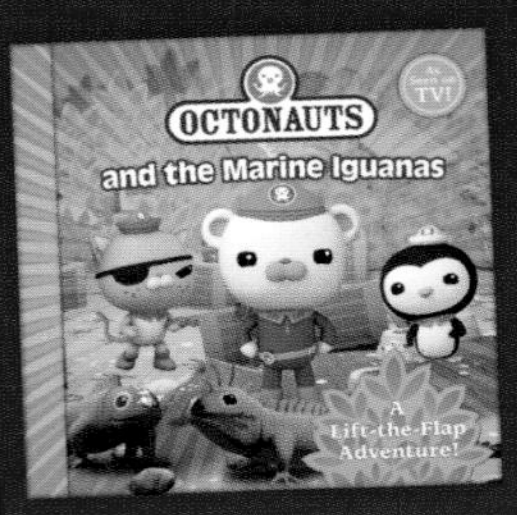

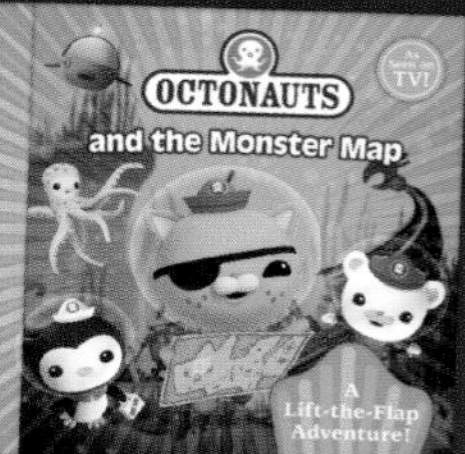

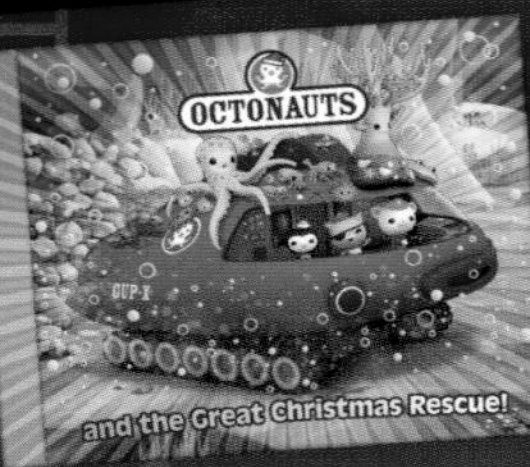

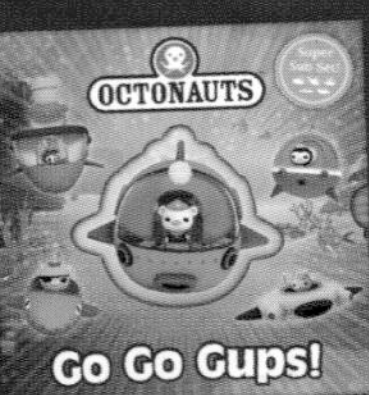

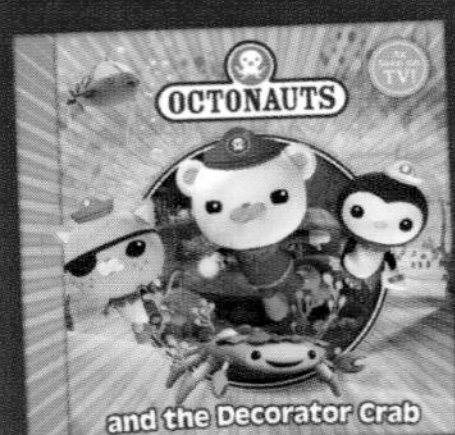

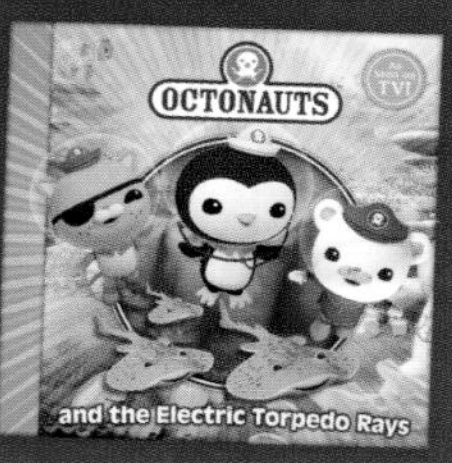

OCTONAUTS Search and Find

www.theOctonauts.com

www.simonandschuster.co.uk